MONSTER HIGH™

HOPES and SCREAMS

MIDLOTHIAN PUBLIC LIBRARY

W9-AKD-866

MIDLOTHIAN PUBLIC LIBRARY

The Monster High™
Gory Gazette™
YOUR UNHH–LTIMATE SOURCE FOR GOSSIP

AN
ORIGINAL
GRAPHIC
NOVEL

BAKER & TAYLOR

WRITTEN BY HEATHER NUHFER · ILLUSTRATED BY JOSH HOWARD

LB
LITTLE, BROWN AND COMPANY
New York Boston

The Monster High
Gory Gazette™
YOUR UHHH-LTIMATE SOURCE FOR GOSSIP

This book is a work of fiction. Names, characters, places, and incidents are the product of the author's imagination or are used fictitiously. Any resemblance to actual events, locales, or persons, living or dead, is coincidental.

Copyright © 2014 Mattel, Inc. All rights reserved. MONSTER HIGH and associated trademarks are owned by and used under license from Mattel, Inc.

Special thanks to Venetia Davie, Tanya Mann, Darren Sander, Julia Phelps, Cindy Ledermann, Garrett Sander, Charnita Belcher, Sharon Woloszyk, and Andrea Isasi.
Cover art by Josh Howard
Cover design by Steve Scott
Interior inks by Josh Howard
Interior colors by Caravan Studio
Bubbles and lettering by Ching Nga Chan

In accordance with the U.S. Copyright Act of 1976, the scanning, uploading, and electronic sharing of any part of this book without the permission of the publisher is unlawful piracy and theft of the author's intellectual property. If you would like to use material from the book (other than for review purposes), prior written permission must be obtained by contacting the publisher at permissions@hbgusa.com.
Thank you for your support of the author's rights.

Little, Brown and Company

Hachette Book Group
237 Park Avenue, New York, NY 10017
Visit our website at lb-kids.com
monsterhigh.com

Little, Brown and Company is a division of Hachette Book Group, Inc.
The Little, Brown name and logo are trademarks of Hachette Book Group, Inc.

The publisher is not responsible for websites (or their content) that are not owned by the publisher.

First Edition: July 2014

Library of Congress Control Number: 2013946010
ISBN 978-0-316-25433-5

10 9 8 7 6 5 4 3 2 1

CW

Printed in the United States of America

MIDLOTHIAN PUBLIC LIBRARY
14701 S. KENTON AVE.
MIDLOTHIAN, IL 60445

The Monster High
Gory Gazette™
YOUR UHHH-LTIMATE SOURCE FOR GOSSIP

TABLE OF CONTENTS

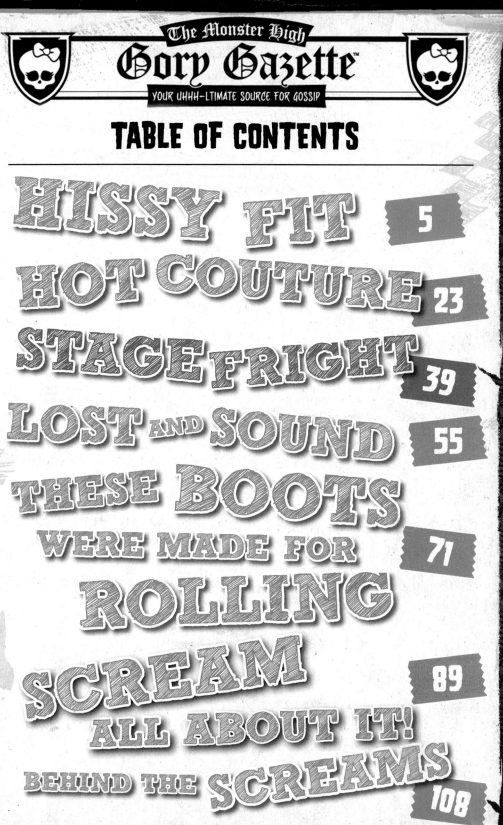

Frankie Stein

Monster Parents: Frankenstein and his bride
Age: How many days has it been?
Frankie is sparking with enthusiasm for unlife at Monster High. She may sometimes fall apart at the seams, but she is always there to lend a helping hand.

Clawdeen Wolf

Monster Parents: The Werewolves
Age: 15
Clawdeen is bold, opinionated, and fiercely loyal to her friends. She is the younger sister of Clawdia and Clawd, and she is Howleen's older sister.

Draculaura

Monster Parents: Dracula
Age: 1,600 years
Draculaura is kind, generous, and scary sweet. She is a vegetarian vampire and a hopeless romantic.

Cleo de Nile

Monster Parents: The Mummy
Age: 5,842 (give or take a few years)
An actual Egyptian princess, Cleo rules the halls of Monster High as captain of the Fear Squad. While a bit self-centered, Cleo is a true friend.

Ghoulia Yelps

Monster Parents: Zombies
Age: 16
Ghoulia may move a bit slowly, but she's the smartest ghoul at Monster High. She speaks only in Zombese, which most monsters can easily understand.

Abbey Bominable

Monster Parents: The Yeti
Age: 16
Abbey is enormously strong and as blunt as a hammer. Her words can come across as cold and harsh, but she has a warm heart.

Robecca Steam

Monster Parents: A Mad Scientist
Age: 116 years
Robecca is a scaredevil, and she loves adventure, particularly those that involve the catacombs.

Howleen Wolf

Monster Parents: The Werewolves
Age: 14
The younger sister of Clawdia, Clawd, and Clawdeen, Howleen is just trying to find her place in the pack.

BOLTS! I GUESS THIS YEAR IS OFF TO A BIG BANG! BEING IN CHARGE OF THE *GAZETTE* IS A BIG DEAL, BUT MAYBE THIS IS *EXACTLY* WHAT THE NEW YEAR HAS IN STORE FOR ME!

DRACULAURA, CLAWDEEN, AND GHOULIA ALREADY WRITE FREAKY-FAB COLUMNS. I KNOW I CAN COUNT ON THEM, BUT WHO ELSE?

CLEO?

SORRY, FRANKIE, I NEED SOME "ME" TIME RIGHT NOW, BUT I'LL HAVE SOMETHING AMAZING TO ADD LATER.

TAP TAP TAP

<YOU COULD THROW AN EPIC PARTY WHEN FRANKIE'S ISSUE IS DONE!>*

GHOULIA, THAT IS BRILLIANT!

*TRANSLATED FROM ZOMBESE

7

WE MUST KEEP THIS A SECRET. I'D BE HUMILIATED. AND I, OF ALL PEOPLE, CANNOT HAVE THAT.

<SEND IN A QUESTION TO DRACULAURA'S ADVICE COLUMN ON THE *GORY GAZETTE*!>

GOLDEN IDEA!

GHOULIA, WRITE ME AN ANONYMOUS POST.

"I'M AFRAID OF SNAKES, AND MY BOYFRIEND'S HEAD IS—" NO, WAIT!

"MY BOYFRIEND HAS A *PET* SNAKE." A PET. NOT SNAKE *HAIR*. "SO I'VE BEEN AVOIDING HIM."

<I'LL JUST EDIT IT A LITTLE BIT.>

GHOULIA! JUST TYPE *EXACTLY* WHAT I SAY! YOU DON'T HAVE TO GO ALL WILLIAM SPOOKSFEAR ON IT!

SIGH!

HOW'S FRANKIE?

YOU SHOULD KNOW.

YEAH, YOU WERE THE ONE MAKING EYES AT FRANKIE, DEUCE.

WHAT?!

BETWEEN MY SNAKES AND THIS, I'LL BE LUCKY IF CLEO EVER SPEAKS TO ME AGAIN!

SO DID HE OR DIDN'T HE?

BLOKES, EH?

AND THEY THINK WE'RE CONFUSING?

19

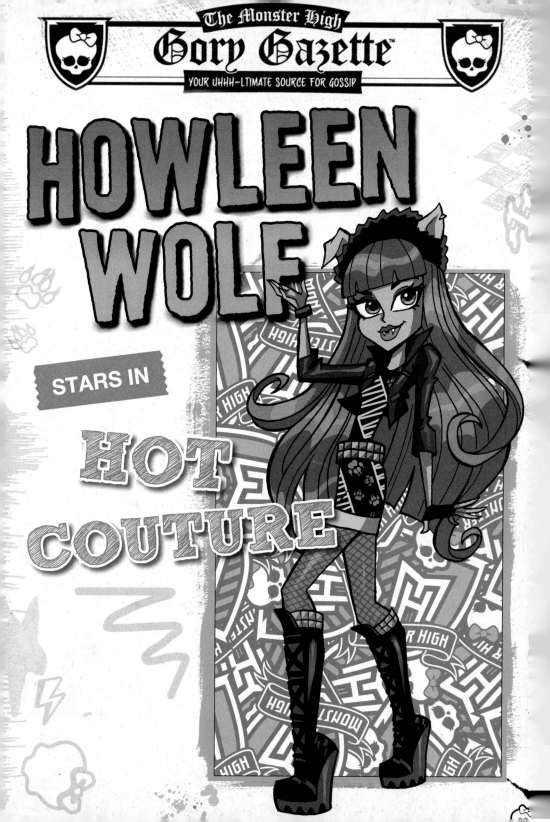

*TRANSLATED FROM ZOMBESE

YAWN!

YAWN!

YAWN!

YAWN!

I CAN'T TAKE THIS KIND OF REJECTION! I NEED YOUR **SISTER'S** HELP.

WE DON'T **NEED** CLAWDEEN FOR ANYTHING! I CAN DO ANYTHING SHE CAN DO, AND BETTER...

...WITH JUST A **LITTLE** HELP FROM HER FASHION SENSE.

NOW **THIS** IS WHAT I'M TALKING ABOUT! WHERE'D YOU COME UP WITH THIS SLAMMIN' ENSEMBLE?

UM, I JUST SCREAMED IT UP, I GUESS....JUST NEED TO MAKE A FEW TWEAKS.

ABBEY WILL LOSE HER MIND WHEN SHE SEES ME IN THIS!

OOOH LA LA! ABBEY?

GULP!

DID I SAY ABBEY? I, UM, MEANT...

NO! NO WAY!

YOU TOTALLY HAVE A CRUSH ON ABBEY! DO YOU WANT TO SKI ON SNOW SLOPES AND DRINK COCOA WITH HER?

hawt!

cute!

WHERE'S EVERYONE GOING?

PEP RALLY! LOOKS LIKE THE NEW LINE IS A HIT! CLAWDEEN IS GOING TO BE STOKED!

HOWLIN' BANSHEES!

FRIGHT

LOOK AT HOLT!

YOU'RE IN A BIG FIELD. A BIG OPEN FIELD. SMELLING OLD GYM SHOES... UGH, IT SMELLS LIKE YAK CHEESE.

CLAWDEEN, YOU'RE A FASHION MAVEN! HOW DO YOU LIKE MY NEW THREADS?

DID A DRAGON ATTACK THE SCHOOL WHILE WE WERE IN HERE?

HA! NO NEED TO BE SO HUMBLE! YOUR DESIGNS ARE ROCK-STAR MATERIAL!

MY DESIGNS?

MY DESIGNS! HOWLEEN!

HOWLEEN. **EXPLAIN.** NOW.

WHOA. SHE'S SO MAD, SHE CAN'T EVEN SPEAK IN COMPLETE SENTENCES!

IT WAS AN ACCIDENT! HEATH WAS ON FIRE AND I—WELL, I JUST WANTED TO BE...SOMETHING!

NOT JUST "CLAWDEEN'S LITTLE SISTER," BUT SOMETHING AS CREEPY-COOL AS YOU!

LISTEN, YOU NEED TO FIND YOUR **OWN** THING TO BE CLAW-SOME AT!

HOW? YOU'RE SO SUPER SCARY AT FASHION, AND CLAWD IS THE CASKETBALL CHAMP....WHAT CAN I DO?

ABBEY! LOOK AT MY KILLER NEW DUDS! I'M THE MOST FASHIONABLE GUY AT SCHOOL!

AH, I SEE. YOU DISAPPEARED TO BECOMING ALL FASHIONABLE LIKE EVERYONE ELSE.

HUH??

EVERYONE'S WEARING THIS LOOK?! OH, MAN! I'M ONLY ONE OF THE MOST FASHIONABLE GUYS AT SCHOOL.

IT'S ONLY FAIR TO MAKE HIM A FASHION SCREAM, RIGHT, CLAWDEEN?

HE DID START THE HOTTEST TREND— LITERALLY.

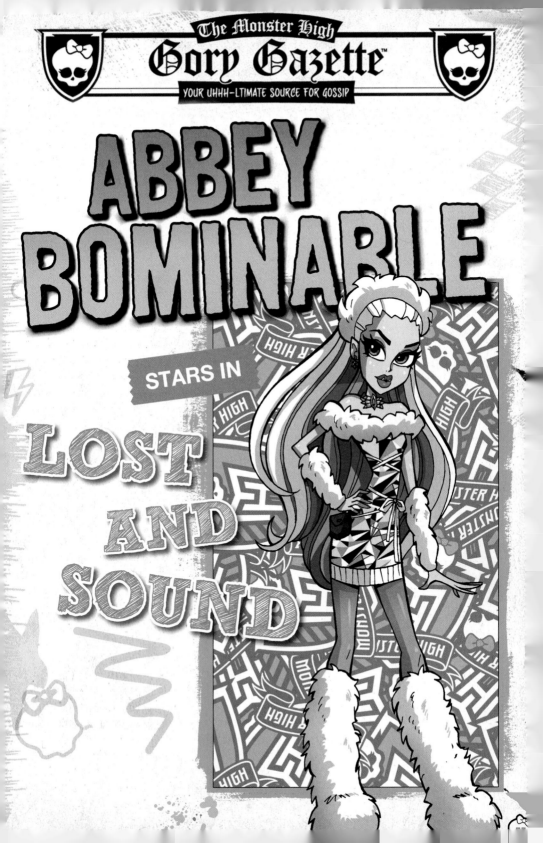

SCRIBBLE SCRIBBLE

SCRIBBLE SCRIBBLE

SIGH. FOR SOME REASON, I JUST CAN'T GET THIS SONG RIGHT.

THANK YOU! ABBEY HAS ALWAYS BEEN GOOD AT FINDING LOST THINGS—EVEN FRIENDSHIP!

YOU PLAY DANCE MIX AT OPENING NIGHT PARTY FOR GORY GAZETTE, YES?

RADICAAAAL!

BZZZZT!

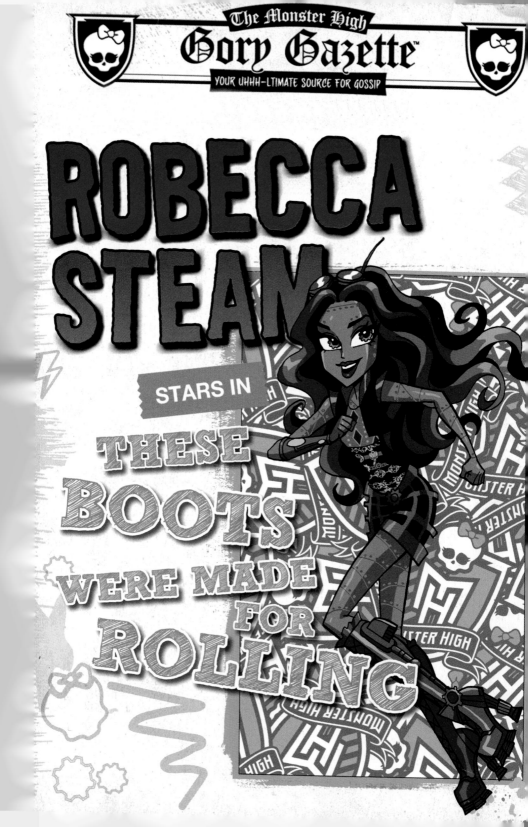

ROBECCA STEAM

STARS IN

THESE BOOTS WERE MADE FOR ROLLING

The Monster High
Gory Gazette ™

YOUR UHHH–LTIMATE SOURCE FOR GOSSIP

FANGTASTIC NEWS   VOLTAGE VOICES   DEAR DRACULAURA   ASK ULA D   SINISTER SPORTS

ARTS AND ENTERTAINMENT   DIG UP THE DIRT   UHHH–ROUND MONSTER HIGH   FURRROCIOUS STYLE

VISIT MONSTERHIGH.COM

Frankie Stein zaps her way to the top

DEAR DRACULAURA

SKRM team glides to victory together!

Gory Gazette Exclusive: Read a brand-new *Dead Fast* story

WORLD PREMIERE VIDEO—
ALL MY MONSTERS!
JUST PRESS PLAY!

Where there's a wolf, there's a way:
Are you a fashion scream?

SCREAM!

For more uhhh-ltimate updates,
check out gorygazette.tumblr.com

BEHIND THE SCREAMS

See how *Hopes and Screams* came to life!

Step 1: rough sketches

Step 2: inks

BEHIND THE SCREAMS

See how *Hopes and Screams* came to life!

Step 3: color

Step 4: balloons and text

ABOUT THE AUTHOR

HEATHER NUHFER

HEATHER NUHFER IS A
SPOOKTACULAR ALL-
AGES WRITER, KNOWN
IN PARTICULAR FOR
HER COMIC-BOOK
WORK, INCLUDING THE
MONSTROUSLY POPULAR
*MY LITTLE PONY: FRIENDSHIP
IS MAGIC*, *STRAWBERRY
SHORTCAKE*, AND *THE
SIMPSONS*. WHEN SHE ISN'T
WRITING, HEATHER LOVES TO
KNIT FREAKY-FAB SWEATERS
FOR HER PUP, EINSTEIN, AND
BAKE TASTY VEGETARIAN
TREATS TO SHARE WITH
DRACULAURA. HER BIGGEST
SCREAM IS TO VISIT SCARIS!

ABOUT THE ILLUSTRATOR

JOSH HOWARD

BORN AND RAISED IN TEXAS, JOSH CAN ALWAYS BE FOUND SCRATCHING AWAY AT HIS LATEST MASTERPIECE UNDER THE LIGHT OF A FULL MOON. HE IS BEST KNOWN AS THE CREATOR OF THE COMIC BOOK *DEAD@17*, AN ACTION/HORROR SERIES ABOUT TEENAGERS, ZOMBIES, SPIRITS, AND GHOULS. (SOUND FAMILIAR?) JOSH IS MARRIED TO A BEAUTIFUL VAMPIRESS NAMED LAURA AND IS THE PROUD FATHER OF THREE LITTLE MONSTERS: LUKE, LONDON, AND WILLOW.

COMING SOON!

The next ghoulgeous
Monster High graphic novel!